For Jacob,
my favorite hat collector

Whose hat?

Whose Hat?

by Margaret Miller

A Mulberry Paperback Book   New York

The photographs were reproduced in full color from 35 mm
Kodachrome slides.
The typeface is Avant Garde Gothic.

Copyright © 1988 by Margaret Miller

The Library of Congress has cataloged the Greenwillow Books
edition of *Whose Hat?* as follows:

Miller, Margaret (date) Whose hat?
Summary: Presents color photographs of hats that represent
various occupations including a chef's cap, construction
worker's helmet, magician's hat, and a fire fighter's hat.
ISBN 0-688-06906-1
ISBN 0-688-06907-X (lib. bdg.)
1. Hats—Juvenile literature. (1. Hats) I. Title.
GT2110.M55 1988 391.'43 86-18324

1 3 5 7 9 10 8 6 4 2
First Mulberry Edition, 1997
ISBN 0-688-15279-1

Chef

Whose hat?

Fire fighter

Whose hat?

Pirate

Whose hat?

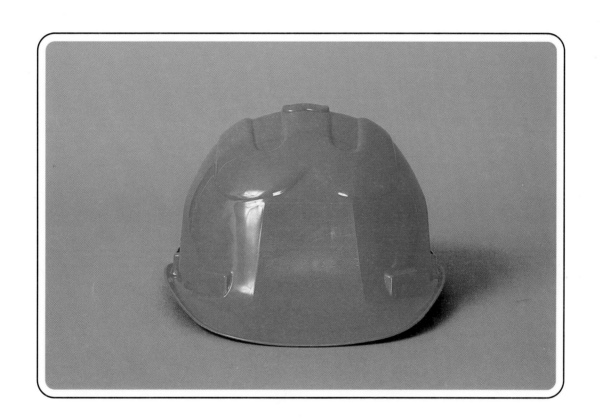

Construction worker

Whose hat?

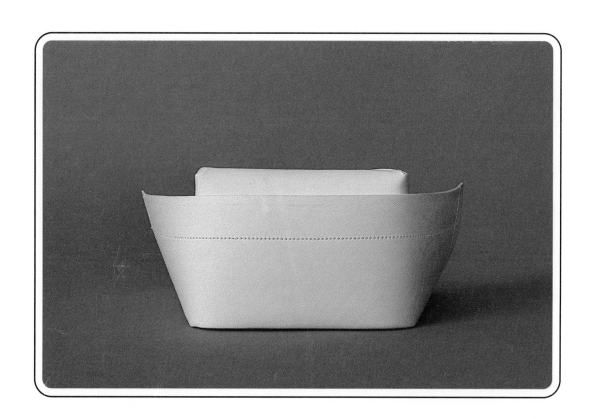

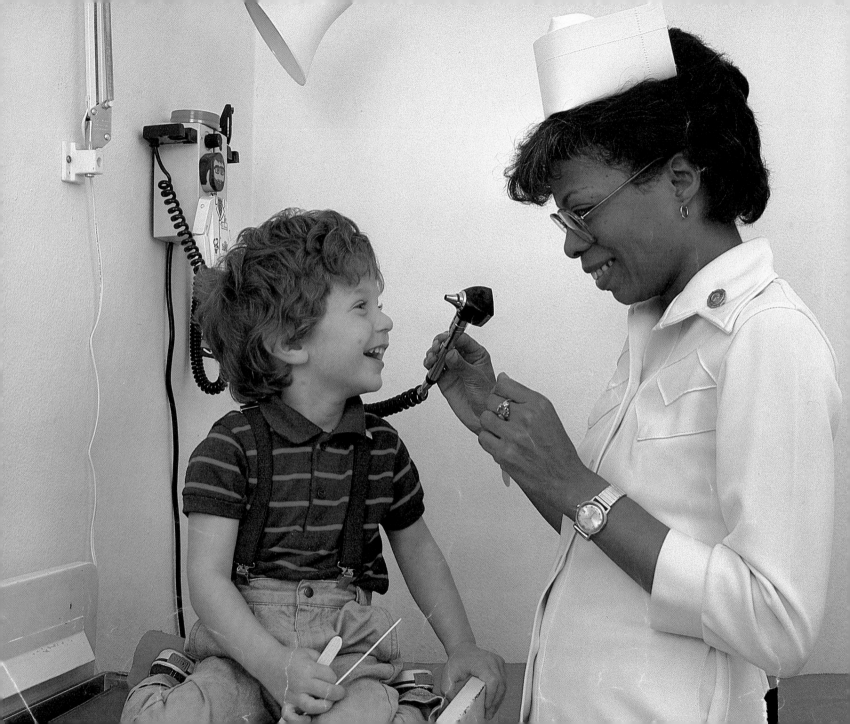

Nurse

Whose hat?

Police
officer

Whose hat ?

Cow hand

Whose hat?

Magician

Whose hat?

Witch

MARGARET MILLER is a freelance photographer who lives in New York City with her husband, two children, two dogs, and many hats. She traces her love of photography to her childhood. "My mother is a wonderful photographer, and as a child I loved being with her in the mysterious darkroom. I also spent many hours looking through two very powerful books, The Family of Man edited by Edward Steichen, and You Have Seen Their Faces by Erskine Caldwell and Margaret Bourke-White. After college I worked in children's book publishing for a number of years, but then took time off to have our two children. As the children grew older and I had more free time, I returned to photography."